Made in the USA
Coppell, TX
19 October 2021

64335400R00056